The Magic Toy Shop

Contributing writer
Carolyn Quattrocki

Cover illustration
Linda Graves

Illustrations
Susan Spellman

Manufactured in U.S.A.

8 7 6 5 4 3 2 1

ISBN: 0-7853-1365-6

PUBLICATIONS INTERNATIONAL, LTD.
Candy Cane Books is a trademark of Publications International, Ltd.

Cornelius was a toymaker who was very busy in his toy shop. "Only two days left before Christmas," he said to himself, "and I still have all these toys to finish. I'm not as young as I used to be, and I can't work as fast. I just hope I'll be able to finish them in time."

The boys and girls couldn't wait to receive their Christmas toys. And Cornelius had made a special one for each child he knew.

That evening Cornelius's wife, Katerina, came into the shop to call him home for his dinner. "I cannot stop now. I must keep on working," said Cornelius, "at least until I finish this toy train. Little Charles will be very disappointed if he doesn't have his train for Christmas."

Cornelius pointed to a princess doll and a pair of skates he had just finished. "At least those are ready for Caroline and little Tommy," he said.

At that moment the toy shop door opened. A poor woman came into the toy shop with her three little children. The children's eyes opened wide as they gazed at all the toys and games.

Peter wished he could have the toy train for his very own. Lisa wanted the beautiful doll. Little Karen wished for the cuddly, pink bunny. But the mother had only a few pennies to spend, and that certainly was not enough for these wonderful toys.

After the poor children and their mother left, Katerina said, "Why don't we give the children the toys that they want, as a special Christmas gift, even if they can't pay for them?"

Cornelius shook his head sadly. "I wish we could, but those toys are already promised. And I have no time to make any others." So the toymaker and his wife closed the shop and went home to their dinner.

After Cornelius and Katerina left, the toys in the little toy shop suddenly came to life! The toys began talking among themselves. They all had heard and seen the poor children wishing for Christmas toys.

Then a toy soldier named Harold had an idea. "We can help. We know more about toys than anyone else does. We can make special Christmas gifts for the children!"

But Louisa, the beautiful doll, said, "What a foolish idea! I've never done any work before, and I will not begin now. You silly toys can go right ahead, but don't count on me!"

She walked over to the corner of the toy shelf and watched as the other toys began to work. Two toy soldiers were already busy putting together the engine of a toy train. And Brown Bear was sewing up the sides of a furry, pink bunny rabbit.

Then Louisa looked up to see two toy kittens trying to paint a face on a princess doll. "My goodness," thought Louisa. "They're making a terrible mess of that doll! Maybe I had better help them, just a little."

Louisa shooed the kittens away and set to work herself. In a while one of the kittens said, "Oooh, how beautiful you have made her—just as beautiful as you!" Louisa smiled and patted the kittens on the head.

When Cornelius and Katerina opened their shop the next day, they saw three toys they had never seen before: a train with a tag that said FOR PETER; a princess doll with a tag that said FOR LISA; and a pink, stuffed bunny whose tag said FOR KAREN. Where had they come from? Something magical must have happened!

That evening Cornelius gave the three children their special, magical Christmas gifts.

Cornelius and Katerina did not go to their shop the next day because it was Christmas. They stayed home to eat their own Christmas dinner.

But the day after Christmas, the old toymaker took down the sign over the door of the toy shop. "I must change the name of my shop," he said. "I will make a new sign. From now on, my shop will not be called THE TOY SHOP. It will be THE MAGIC TOY SHOP!"

Cornelius and Katerina were very proud that such a magical thing had happened in their shop. They could hardly wait until next Christmas—the most magical holiday of the year!